Carnival
An imprint of the Children's Division
of the Collins Publishing Group
8 Grafton Street, London W1X 3LA

Published by Carnival 1988

Count Duckula is a registered trademark of THAMES TELEVISION plc.
Copyright © COSGROVE HALL PRODUCTIONS 1988

ISBN 0 00 194513 0

Printed and bound in Great Britain by
Collins, Glasgow

The Count Duckula Storybook

Adapted by Maureen Spurgeon
from original Cosgrove Hall Productions scripts
by Peter Richard Reeves and directed by Chris Randall

CARNIVAL

THAMES

1
Transylvanian Homesick Blues

Deep in the heart of the dark, brooding Transylvanian Alps, the towers of Castle Duckula stretch up to the sky, almost like skeleton hands casting their black shadows on the earth below.

Nobody stirs in this terrible place. No voices echo through the lonely castle walls, to tell of the evil vampire barons whose home Castle Duckula has been for centuries.

Sometimes, wayfarers may talk of mankind being saved from these monsters with a lust for human blood, of the vampire being slain by a stake through the heart, or a beam of sunlight shining into mad, staring eyes . . .

But, none dare speak of the dreadful secret ritual which can only be performed once every hundred years, and which brings the vampire master, Count Duckula, back to life!

And all around there is a grim silence, broken only by the dismal creaking of a gate with a sign on it . . .

So often Igor, the gloomy-faced manservant at Castle Duckula, wondered what could possibly have gone wrong at the last vampire ritual . . .

Whoever heard of a vampire who was scared of the sight of blood, Igor asked himself yet again, with a secret shudder. All his young master ever seemed to eat was broccoli sandwiches made by that fool of an old Nanny. Why, he even told people he was a vegetarian . . . Vegetarian! Igor could still hardly believe it.

Then there was Castle Duckula, able to transport itself anywhere in the world on command of the master. Igor well remembered the Duckulas using it to collect rare and vintage blood groups on many a delightful occasion . . .

Still, he reflected darkly, at least he had managed to talk the Count out of travelling by Castle to a fun-fair. That would have ruined the family name completely . . .

But Igor was mistaken. The castle had transported whilst he was thinking and had indeed arrived at a fun-fair.

"Roll up, roll up!" bawled a voice, interrupting Igor's morbid thoughts. "This way for Doctor Fazackerly Tyme's roller coaster! Travel in time! Be the envy of your friends!"

"Wow! Sounds fabulous, doesn't it? If it is anything like those dodgems we've just been on, it'll be great," breathed Duckula, yellow beak wide open in amazement. "Go and get the tickets, Igor!"

Igor opened his mouth to protest – but Duckula and Nanny were already boarding the roller coaster, and getting strapped into their seats.

"This is Doctor Fazackerly Time!" the captain greeted from the cockpit. "Our cruising height is a complete mystery, speed will be quite fast, and the destination none of your business!"

Then the engines gave one last, deafening roar, Doctor Tyme's clock chimed – and the roller coaster was off on its journey!

"This is what I call travelling!" cried Duckula, scenery whizzing by so fast that everything was soon a blur. "When do we get to where we're going, Doctor Tyme?"

"When I find the brake!" came the reply. Duckula gave a horrified gulp, but Doctor Tyme seemed too busy looking vaguely around to notice. "I put it in a cardboard box, somewhere . . ."

"Ooh! Is this what you want, Doctor?" cried Nanny, making herself useful for once and handing it over.

"Most kind, my dear!" Doctor Tyme smiled at her. "You can call me Fazackerly!"

"Oooh. . .!" squealed Nanny. "You naughty doctor, you!"

"I hate to break this up," Count Duckula interrupted, "but we seem to be going nowhere fast!"

"Have no fear!" Doctor Tyme declared, taking the brake out of the box and giving it a tug. "Time is on our side! Ha-ha-ha!"

The roller coaster juddered to a halt, jerking them all forward. Nanny was the first to get her breath, gazing around at a desert wilderness, with only a few live volcanoes and some dinosaurs in sight . . .

"The beach!" she exclaimed joyfully. "You know, I haven't been to the seaside for years!"

"There doesn't appear to be any sea, Milord!" murmured Igor.

"Tide's probably out, Igor!" explained Count Duckula. He thought he sounded rather clever – until Doctor Tyme broke in:

"If it is out, then it will take some time to come back in again! This is prehistoric earth, a million years before you were born!"

"A million years?" gasped Nanny. "But I left the dinner in the oven!"

"No need to get upset, Nanny!" Duckula told her. "We'll get back to Transylvania – won't we, Doctor?"

"Not if I have anything to do with it!" rumbled a deep voice out of nowhere. And Doctor Tyme still had his mouth closed!

"What was that?" Duckula wondered aloud. The only answer was a sinister creaking – which the Count thought he recognised.

"Is that your stomach playing up again, Igor?"

Igor said nothing. His huge, ugly old eyes bulged out of his bony old head as the lid of a stone coffin creaked even louder, then flew open to reveal . . . a Stone Age vampire, complete with fur cape.

"Aha!" he cried, leaping out with enthusiasm. "Aha!"

"Aha?" echoed Duckula in scorn. Even as a vegetarian vampire duck, he felt he could do better. "You can't just have Aha! It doesn't make sense!"

"Look, I am the world's first vampire!" snarled the vampire, baring his fangs to prove it. "How do I know Aha! doesn't make sense!"

Igor gave a polite cough. "I was wondering why Sir is out in the middle of the day."

"Why?" asked the vampire, quite interested. "Is that wrong?"

"Oh, completely, Sir. You should only come out at night!"

"Night?" echoed the vampire in surprise. "But you can't see a thing then!"

A painful wince and a few shudders – and Igor was ready to try again.

"Have you tried sinking you teeth into something, yet, Sir?"

"Ah, yes!" said the vampire, cheering up. "I tried that for the first time this morning!"

"Everything went well, I trust, Sir? The victim was very tasty?"

"Victims . . ." repeated the vampire, suddenly thoughtful. "So that's what they're called . . . Anyway, it wasn't very tasty, now you mention it. And it's been chasing me ever since! In fact . . ." he went on, his vampire tones rising to a yell, "here comes that victim again!"

And he dived straight back into his stone coffin to escape a gigantic dinosaur – which continued charging forwards, making the entire prehistoric desert rumble!

"Quick, Milord!" yelled Igor. He didn't much fancy dinosaurs, either. "We must get away!"

"Don't you worry, my dear," Doctor Tyme was saying, ushering Nanny towards the roller coaster.

"I can tell you're a doctor!" she puffed. "You've got such nice hands!"

"He won't have a nice anything if that thing catches up with us, Nanny!" Count Duckula pointed out. "Let's get out of here!"

They hardly remembered scrambling into the roller coaster, before it surged away again, zooming along so fast that all of them could feel their faces being pulled to the backs of their heads!

"At least time travel pushes the wrinkles away where nobody sees them, Igor!" pronounced Duckula, once the roller coaster had come to a stop. "Now, are we all here? Igor, the doc, me – yes, I'm, here – and, Nanny . . . Nanny!" he bawled at her. "I asked if you're here!"

"I'm engaged . . ." sighed Nanny, gazing dreamily into Doctor Tyme's eyes. "The Doctor has just proposed . . ."

"Engaged?" spluttered Duckula. He could hardly believe his ears. "But, Nanny, think of the problems – the-the expense, the people we'll have to invite to the wedding . . .!"

"Excuse me, Sir," interrupted Igor solemnly, "but I'd like to point out we are being watched by a potato!"

"A potato?" echoed Duckula. "Well he won't get an invitation, unless he's a close friend of the bride, or . . ." He paused uncertainly. "Er, did you say – potato, Igor?"

"Yes, Sir. A giant potato – with rather a nasty look on its face, Sir!"

Count Duckula was about to suggest that even potatoes have their bad days – when the potato stepped right up to him, closely followed by lots of other potatoes.

"Who is it that trespasses on our land?" it demanded, potato eyes boring straight into Duckula.

"I am Count Duckula!" he began grandly, "The great peace-maker, noted vegetar . . ." The potato eyes bored even deeper. "And – and a vegetable's friend!"

"You are all strangers!" pronounced Potato, whilst various other vegetables joined him. "Not unlike those from the old times, before the vegetables began to rule!"

"Vegetables in power?" gasped Duckula. "Where are we, Doc?"

"About 4008!" informed Doctor Tyme. "If I remember correctly, an artichoke has just been made President of the United States, and two cucumbers have landed on Venus!"

"A cucumber on Venus . . ." murmured Duckula. "One small step for man, but a giant leap for the salad bar!"

"One other thing," added Doctor Tyme. "They are all meat-eaters, and their favourite food is – duck!"

"Duck!" exclaimed the Count, his beak beginning to chatter. "Oh, really. . ?"

"Are you a duck?" demanded the potato.

"Me?" Duckula tried to laugh, then coughed instead. "No, no! I'm a marrow, aren't I, Igor?"

"Oh, most definitely, Sir!"

"Then, why is it you have feathers?"

"Er – feathered marrows are quite the thing!" gabbled Duckula
desperately. "Like woolly cucumbers or hairy bananas! Isn't that right,
Nanny?" There was no answer. "Nanny!" shrieked Duckula. "Igor, where's
Nanny?"

A strangled cry broke from Igor's thin lips, his trembling forefinger
pointing into the distance. "Doctor Tyme's roller coaster! It's leaving
without us! Run for it, Milord!"

"Sieze them!" screamed the potato. "Have them scraped and boiled and
served with a little butter!"

Even as Igor and Count Duckula ran, Nanny was grieving for her young
master.

"Oooh, Doctor," she kept wailing, twisting her podgy hands in her lap.
"Where's my little Duckyboos?"

A sinister smile spread across the Doctor's face as the roller coaster
began picking up speed. "With any luck," he said, "roasting very nicely!"

15

"You monster!" burst out Nanny, kicking and punching him with her bad arm. "I could never marry anyone who had my lovely duck eaten! He was kind and brave and strong and all the things you're not!"

"Know something, Igor?" croaked Duckula from the back seat. "I think she means it . . ."

"She didn't say anything about me, Sir," Igor reflected darkly. But Nanny was already turning around and reaching out towards them with her one good arm.

"Oo I liked you too, Mister Igor!" she cooed delightedly. "You're safe! And my Duckyboos!"

"So!" snarled Doctor Tyme, landing the roller coaster with a bump. "You would spurn me, would you, my little chicken? Then I shall have my revenge!"

"Aristos!" he bellowed out loud. "I have caught some aristos!"

And, within seconds, they were surrounded by crowds of angry citizens from the French Revolution!

"Yes, take them away!" cried Doctor Tyme, watching the crowds surging towards Nanny, Igor and Duckula. "Clap them in irons!"

Before long, they were all thrown into a cell in the famous Bastille. Nanny, Igor, Count Duckula and, . . . Doctor Tyme . . . much to Duckula's amusement.

"Bad luck, Doc! You weren't to know they were arresting everybody in funny outfits as well!"

"I should have been prepared . . ." said Tyme. "I could have worn the pinstripe trousers with the black jacket!"

"We'll have to escape!" Count Duckula decided, thinking hard. "I know! When the guard comes with our dinner – let him have it!"

Nanny was most alarmed. "What are we going to eat?"

"He means, let him have it on the head with something heavy, hard and horrible, Nanny!" Igor explained patiently. "One of your soufflés would have been ideal!"

"That's all right, then!" said Nanny, delving into her sling. "I always carries a soufflé in case of emergencies!"

"That's great, Nanny!" cried Duckula, holding out both hands. Nanny, of course, missed completely, and down went the soufflé, thudding on the cell floor like a cannonball. "Let's hope we can lift it . . ."

Duckula struggled up on top of Igor, behind the door and tried to keep hold of Nanny's soufflé at the same time. It was hard work, especially when Igor was standing on Doctor Tyme's shoulders, too. But, with a lot of puffing and heaving, they finally managed it, only seconds before there was a great rattling of keys outside the door . . .

"On your foots!" roared the guard, flinging back the door – and flattening them against the wall in a chorus of groans. "By order of the people's revolution, you are to have your heads removed from your bodies . . ."

He certainly wasn't expecting a blow on his own head from Nanny's sling!

"The door's open, Milord!" hissed Igor. "We must escape!"

They had hurried through a long chamber, past the menacing shadow of the guillotine, before another guard bellowed: "Queek! Queek! After them!"

But Duckula, Igor and Nanny were scrambling aboard the roller coaster before the French had got very far, Doctor Tyme leaping into the cockpit without saying another word until they landed back at the fairground.

"Bother!" he said, looking at his time clock. "Five minutes early!"

Duckula let out a deep breath. "Phew! That was some dodgem ride, Igor! I – feel sort of dizzy . . ."

"Roll up, roll up!" cried a voice. "This way for Doctor Fazackerly Tyme's roller coaster! Travel in time! Be the envy . . ."

"Wow-ee---!" breathed Duckula "Sounds fabulous, doesn't it, Nanny? If it is anything like those dodgems we've just been on it'll be great."

"Hmm . . ." Nanny murmured. "Funny, but I've got a feeling we've been through all this before."

2
The Mutinous Penguins

There is no human on earth who can say when the terrible foundations of Castle Duckula were laid . . . Nor when its black towers first stretched towards the dark skies of Transylvania.

Hushed whispers tell of the evil power within the Castle walls – power to transport the building itself on command of its vampire master. A secret, only Count Duckula dares to speak of . . .

"Come in, Igor, stop leaning over the side! You're supposed to be looking for the Castle! Any sign of it, yet?"

"No, Sir," his manservant responded miserably. "Only icebergs, Sir, and-and the sea going up and down, and up, and . . ."

"We're lucky to have found this ship, you know!" Duckula scolded. "Igor, how could you lose a whole castle!"

"Me, Sir?" croaked Igor, swallowing hard. "Nanny probably let the safety catch off!"

"Oh, yes!" Duckula yelled at him. "It's easy to blame poor old Nanny!"

"Yes – it's very easy to blame Nanny," agreed Igor.

"Okay," said Duckula. "We'll do that then."

The deck rumbled with the unearthly din of crashing and smashing below, before the hatch door was thrown open, and Nanny emerged in her usual state of confusion.

"Did you call, Duckyboos?" she puffed. "Ooh, I'll be glad to get home, making tea in my own kitchen!"

"Well, we've got to find the castle, first!" snapped Duckula. "Go and have a word with the captain, Igor!"

"I only wish, Sir," said Igor, "I could feel happier about the crew . . ."

The captain didn't seem too friendly, either, when Igor showed him Duckula's map. "By my calculations," he said, pointing a finger, "Castle Duckula should be just there!"

"Flip my flippers!" cackled the captain. "That be the South Seas!"

"So, are we on course?" Duckula persisted. "Is the ship all ship-shape? All hands ready for inspection?"

"That's right, Duckyboos!" twittered Nanny. "See they've got nice, clean fingernails!"

"Quiet, Nanny!" ordered Count Duckula. "We're searching for the castle!"

"But, Ducky," Nanny quavered, "if we just wait . . ."

"Be quiet, Nanny!" thundered Duckula, red in the beak.

Nanny turned away, muttering to herself. "All right . . . Don't wait for the castle to come back by itself, and don't say I didn't tell you, 'cos I didn't . . ."

But Nanny never liked any kind of upset with her Duckyboos. So, before long, she went along to his cabin where he and Igor were working together on the map.

"Coo-ee, Ducky Darling!" she called. "Look what Nanny's brought you!"

"Nanny!" Count Duckula beamed. "That should make a great chandelier!!" Then he examined the peace-offering more slowly. "Er, haven't I seen this before?"

"More than likely, Sir!" agreed Igor, grimly. "It's the ship's wheel!"

"You-you mean," gulped Duckula in horror, "there's nothing to steer the ship? Aaaagh! Help! Captain! Captain!"

The captain, however, was already talking to his crew . . .

"This trip ain't to find no castle, lads! I reckon that duck's after buried treasure in the South Seas! Now, suppose we was to capture him and his chums . . ."

"We'd have to be cunning about it, though . . ." growled the ship's mate. "I mean, we can't expect them to rush up here, and . . ."

"Help!" Duckula shouted again, and the door burst open. "Captain! We're in your hands!"

"Well, well . . ." murmured the captain with a secret smile. "Life's full of surprises . . ."

"Captain," Igor broke in, with a respectful bow. "I believe you've mislaid this!"

"Shiver me timbers! That's the ship's wheel you've nicked! Tie 'em to the yard arm, men!"

"I ate the yard arm last week, Captain," announced the mate, somewhat sheepishly. "There's only the comfy sofa left!"

"Tie 'em to the comfy sofa?" spluttered the captain in disbelief. "I can't say that!"

"You just did, captain!"

"Oh, all right!" exclaimed the captain in exasperation. "Tie 'em to the comfy sofa! Then go and get that treasure map!"

"Snow-covered tropical island on the port bow, Sir!" bellowed a sailor from the crow's nest. The captain rubbed his flippers together. "Aha!" he cackled. "This is where you get off, me hearties! Throw 'em overboard, lads!"

With some difficulty, the crew nudged the sofa towards the end of a long plank – until it plummeted down on to a huge ice floe with a resounding crack, and a loud "Ow-ow-ow!" from Nanny.

Duckula and Igor thanked their lucky stars she was heavy enough, and clumsy enough, to break both the sofa and theirs bonds as they landed!

"You rats!" bellowed Duckula, as the ship sailed out of sight. "You skunks! You – you . . ."

Nanny gave a good-natured chuckle. "Come on now, my Duckyboos! How about a nice cup of tea!"

"Oh, yes?" Duckula scoffed at her. "And a crumpet, I suppose?"

Nanny began searching frantically in her sling. "Wait a minute, dear!" she cooed. "Just let me get the stove out, and my tea-pot, then we'll see . . . Ah!" Something gold winked in the wintry sunshine. "Here we are!"

"Nanny!" groaned Duckula. "I said crumpet, not trumpet!"

"Allow me to light the stove," Igor offered hastily, flipping his thumb and forefinger together to produce the necessary flame.

Altogether, it was rather a nice little tea-party, with cakes and sandwiches, and the tea-pot steaming cosily. It was a shame no one noticed that the stove had begun to melt a huge wall of ice, making it crackle quite alarmingly.

Suddenly, Igor gave a polite cough. "I believe we have visitors, Sir!"

"Visitors!" spat out Duckula, gulping down the last of his sandwich. "Just as we're having tea! Tell 'em to wait in the library – visitors! Gulp!"

"Quite, Sir. But they – ahem! – appear to have come through the wall . . ."

Viking helmets, complete with horns . . . shields . . . spears . . . big feet . . . thick muscles . . . These visitors certainly looked strong enough to come through any wall, Duckula decided, trying hard to stop his cloak shaking.

"Er – would you like a muffin?" he stammered, but the Vikings didn't seem to understand. Instead they went into an elaborate mime routine, which only Igor could make any sense of.

"Is it a film?" he queried, concentrating hard. "Book? History! Frozen mice? No, no! Frozen ice, that's it!"

"It appears, Milord, that these gentlemen discovered the North Pole a thousand years ago. They were preserved in the ice – until Nanny's tea revived them! I always said she could waken the dead!"

"Ooh, thank you, Mister Igor!" cried Nanny. "What are they saying, now?"

"They want us to follow them," said Igor, "and bring the tea-pot!" Duckula suddenly gave a shriek of panic-stricken horror.

"This island's shrinking! Look, Nanny's stove thing is melting the ice! Quick, Igor, do something!"

Much to their surprise, they felt something lifting them high in the air – and the next minute, they were sliding down on to the deck of a submarine!

"Who is zat, tap-dancing on my roof?" someone grumbled, and Doctor Von Goosewing, the famous vampire-catcher, began fussing around. "No peace, even at der North Pole! Now, my sonar vampire-radar iz telling me a vampire castle nearby iz . . ."

He squinted into his periscope – only to see a face which he knew very well indeed looking back down at him!

"Aaaagh! It is Count Dugula! Full speed ahead!"

"Hold on to the submarine tower!" screamed Duckula. "There's an iceberg straight ahead!"

There was a shuddering bang, and Von Goosewing's submarine crashed, throwing them all out in a heap. They all slipped and slid along quite a distance before they came to a great ice cavern, where the Viking Chief pointed soundlessly to a huge block of ice.

"Do you see what I see?" breathed Duckula. "There, in the ice? Looks like a Viking Queen . . ."

"Quite so, Milord," agreed Igor, glancing around to see the Viking Chief beginning his mime act once more. "And, it appears, they want . . ."

"I know!" cooed Nanny, taking a steaming kettle from her sling. "A fresh pot coming right up!"

Some hot water, a quick stir – and the ice block started to melt. The Viking Queen burst into song at once.

"I am fre-e-e--eeee!" she squealed. "At last, I am free-eee-!"

Duckula winced. "Somehow," he said, "I get the feeling we should have left her in the ice-pack!"

"Tell me, little yellow nose," beamed the Viking Queen, "how can I reward you for my freedom?"

"Well . . ." replied Duckula, after some thought, "you could help us find that penguin crew, and get our map back . . ."

The Viking Queen didn't need asking twice. "Men of the north, away, away!" she warbled. "Take the long-boat from the freezer!"

A long-boat rowed by Vikings and carrying Duckula, Igor, Nanny AND a Viking Queen was the last thing the pirate penguins expected to see coming after them!

"Avast there, ye lubbers!" thundered the Captain. "Go away, or we'll blow you out of the water . . ."

The crew took aim – but found it was very difficult – a submarine was blocking their view.

"Have any of you seen a vampire castle?" enquired Von Goosewing from the direction of the hatch. "It's sort of big, and sinister, and . . ."

He ducked down sharply, just missing a cannonball whizzing past his head. "Chee! I vas only a polite question asking –"

"Let the penguins and the Vikings sort it out!" Duckula hissed across to Nanny and Igor. "This is our chance to escape! Jump!" There was no time to argue. Together, the three of them jumped into Von Goosewing's submarine. Duckula went straight to the controls.

"Hurry!" he snarled, hoping he sounded like a Hollywood gangster. "Get under the water!"

"Hi-jacked!" wailed Goosewing, his dusty glasses sliding down the end of his crooked nose. "By a vampire duck!"

"Ooh, look!" cried Nanny, gazing out of a port-hole. "That's just like our dining room!"

"Nanny," said Duckula slowly, "you do not find dining rooms under water. And, what's more . . ." he added, then gave a whoop of joy, "Hey, Igor! Look! We've found the castle!"

Igor's solemn eyes widened dramatically. Von Goosewing's submarine was actually floating through Castle Duckula!

"Quick, Goosewing!" ordered Duckula. "Surface!"

Von Goosewing had no choice. The submarine rose up through the castle into one of the top floor rooms, where Nanny, and Igor and Duckula clambered out thankfully, stamping all over Goosewing's equipment as they did so.

"Ach, now mine Vampireometer is all squished to little pieces," complained Goosewing, as the submarine dived out of sight. "Chust vait till it's fixed, I'll get ze lot of you!"

There was more trouble on the horizon when Igor and Duckula opened the windows. Trouble, that is, in the shape of penguins charging the castle with bits of pirate ship, and angry Vikings fast approaching, brandishing swords and the remnants of their long-boat!

Count Duckula covered his eyes. "This is it!" he wailed. "The line of the Duckulas is finished!"

"You might be saved by the bell, Milord," suggested Igor, cupping a hand to his ear. "Or, should it be the cuckoo?"

"Cuckoo! Cuckoo!" chirped the Duckula clock obligingly, ready to power Castle Duckula into flight with an increasingly loud rumble.

"You see, Duckyboos?" said Nanny. "The castle always comes back on its own!"

"At dawn, Eastern Transylvania Standard time, Milord!" remembered Igor, clutching his forehead in exasperation.

"I apologise, Nanny!" said Duckula. "If only I'd listened to you in the first place!"

"Well, now we're here, in this place," beamed Nanny, "what about a nice cup of tea?"

The peasants of Transylvania imagined they heard the dreadful cries of the werewolf as it stalked its prey through the night.

But, it was only Nanny singing to herself as she put the kettle on . . .

3
One
Stormy Night

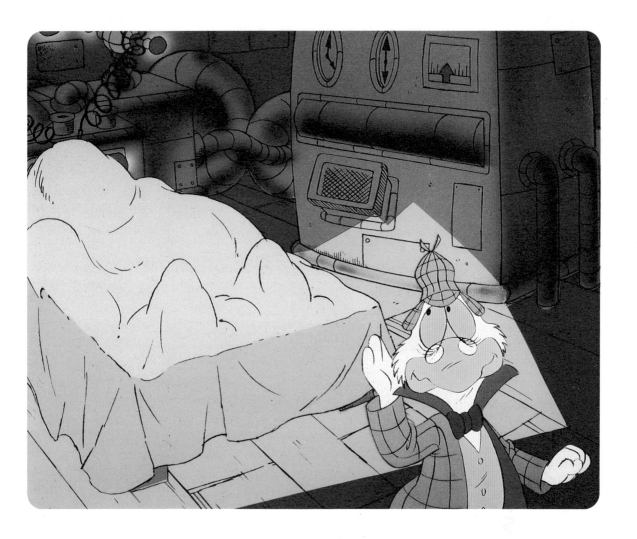

There is nowhere more sinister, more terrifying, than Castle Duckula on a dark, stormy night . . . tormented shadows brought to life by jagged fingers of lightning . . . winds howling through the trees, thunder crashing to the depths of the cold Transylvanian earth . . .

And, within Castle Duckula itself, there came a new threat to the most dreaded of all vampires, Count Duckula . . .

"Ach, mine own little baby!" Doctor Von Goosewing, the noted vampire catcher, was gazing proudly at his creation. Every five minutes, he would go to the stone slab where it lay covered by a sheet, and speak comfortingly. "Soon, ze thunderbolt will be caught by mine machine, unt you will live! Zen, together, we will destroy ze house of Dugula!"

"Zat is," he added, "if I can fix ze fuse-box! Hang on ein second, while I get ze fuse! Zat's the trouble with havink mein laboratory hidden secretly in zis place."

Claps of thunder hid the sound of his footsteps as he began creeping around the castle – not too far from Duckula's bedroom, where Igor was reading a bed-time story.

"And the great ugly thing strode across Transylvania, eating houses, roads, swamps, food mixers and blenders . . ."

"Hey, Igor!" broke in Count Duckula, his blue night-cap almost falling off. "All this stuff about eating is making me peckish!"

"Oooh, Duckyboos!" wailed Nanny. "How can you think of eating with that horrid creature destroying the world?"

"*The Thing That Ate Transylvania*? It's only a story, Nanny!"

There was a deafening crash of thunder, bouncing off Goosewing's machinery and on through every floor in the castle, until it reached the dungeons with a final, terrifying bang, revitalising the effigy on the tomb of one of Duckula's ancestors.

"Oooh, love us!" screamed Nanny, taking a flying leap into Igor's arms. "What was that?"

"That, Nanny," growled Duckula, "was my stomach telling me that I need a snack! You calm down and I'll go and get it!"

"Oooh, no! Don't leave me here on my own!"

"Igor's here, Nanny!" Duckula reminded her, watching a pair of trouser-legs rapidly descending through fast-splintering floorboards. "He may not be much company at the moment, but . . ."

"Aaaagh!" moaned Igor, and completely vanished through the hole in the floor, finally out-weighed and defeated by Nanny's bulk.

Down, down he fell, floor by floor, only coming to a halt in a dungeon tomb, with the lid slamming down on top of him.

"Ah!" breathed Duckula, after a pause. "He's not here, after all! I suppose you'd better come with me, Nanny!"

Still the storm raged around Castle Duckula, lightning now flashing on a terrible, grey figure, the very essence of wickedness, gazing around the dungeons . . .

"How wonderful!" the voice rasped chillingly through its grey beak, black vampire cloak floating behind like enormous bat wings. "On such a night, we Duckulas can be nothing but completely evil! Ha-ha-ha."

He drew his cape across his face, ready to pounce on the first person who dared approach . . .

"Ah, younk lady!" cried Goosewing. "You look like just ze person to hef unt fuse . . ."

"Fuse?" came the reply. "I have the very thing in the dung . . . I mean, the cellar! Follow me, won't you?"

A flash of lightning forked through the window of Goosewing's laboratory, bouncing into the machinery and bringing his monster to life.

One last flash, one final ripple of movement beneath the sheet, and the creature sat up, raising a hand to feel the rusty bolt through its much-stitched head.

"Oooh . . ." winced the monster, clanking its great feet on the floor. "I would have to wake up vis a headache! Unt my mouth feels like the bottom of a trash-can!"

Very gingerly, he felt around Goosewing's wire stitching. "Oh . . ." he sighed. "It *is* the bottom of a trash-can! I would hef to be made from metal! *Nobody* likes metal . . ."

There was another crash of thunder, making the monster clutch at his head once more.

"Oooh!" he groaned, stumbling towards the door. "What I need is ein aspirin!"

Meanwhile, Nanny and Count Duckula were making their way down to the kitchen.

"There you are, Nanny!" Duckula was saying, waving a hand at the shadowy walls. "Absolutely no monsters. Not one single monster in sight!"

"But," faltered Nanny, "it could be anywhere, eating away walls and cupboards and all sorts of stuff . . ."

"Eating away at all sorts of stuff!" repeated Duckula. "That's just what I'm going to be doing in a minute! Come on, Nanny! Snackwards!"

"Oooh, no!" Nanny held tight to the bannisters. "I'm not going downstairs! Supposing the monster's down there?"

Duckula opened his beak to protest, then shut it tight and gave a deep sigh instead. "All right, Nanny," he said, "you go upstairs!"

"Why?"

"Because if the monster's downstairs, he can't be upstairs, can he?"

Nanny gave up. "All right, Master Duckula. But if I get eaten, I'm handing in my notice!"

Without Nanny, Duckula clattered down the stairs quite jauntily, never dreaming that his grey double was, at that very moment, leading Von Goosewing through the maze of dungeons!

"There are dozens of fuses over here, my friend!" he sniggered. "Hurry!"

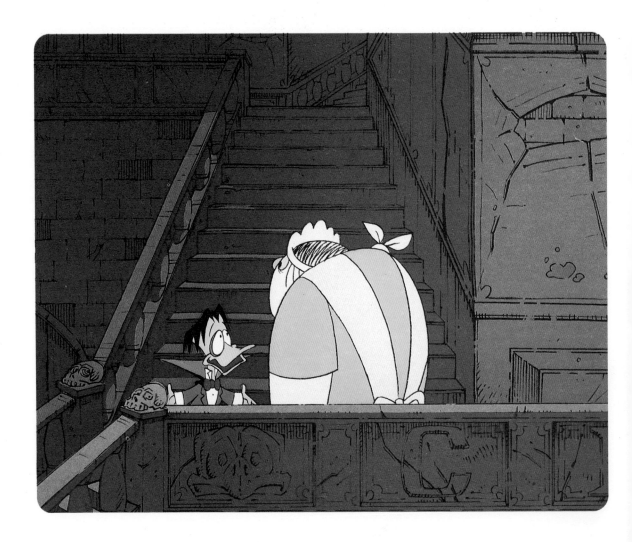

"I'm goink as fast as I can!" protested Goosewing, peering through his dusty spectacles at a tall, black shadow looming ahead, a dull gleam coming from the triangular blade at the top . . .

"The fuse is there," directed the grey effigy pointing a long fingernail. "In the basket!"

Everything seemed to be working better than he dared hope! There was Goosewing, actually putting his bumbling head through the guillotine to look into the basket . . . he only had to pull the rope to release the blade . . .

"Just a little closer . . ." he muttered, his voice rising with excitement. "That's it! Blood! I love it! Eee! Gore!"

The lid of the stone tomb flew back with a resounding thud. "Did you call, Master?" asked Igor, thinking he had heard his name.

"Master?" echoed Von Goosewing, jerking his head back from the guillotine, only seconds before the blade slammed down and running off. "Zo! Iss you, Dugula! I will get mine monster, and destroy you!"

"You fool!" the effigy rapped out at Igor. "You ruined a perfectly good meal! And I was hoping you'd help me do a little evil tonight . . ."

As the manservant to a long line of most distinguished vampires, Igor was delighted. "After all my hard work!" he murmured happily, clasping his hands and thinking it was Count Duckula. "I think he's got it!"

"Our little Von Goosewing friend . . ." Duckula's born-again ancestor was saying, "we'll roast him over a warm spoon, then bury him out the back!"

"Oh, master – a packed lunch! How clever!"

"So, fetch me a spade! Tonight is our really nasty night!"

It was a really tiring night for Nanny, who had exhausted herself climbing all the stairs to get away from the monster.

"Oooh, look," she panted, peering into Von Goosewing's laboratory. "A nice place to lie down . . ."

True, the table sagged and groaned beneath her weight. But Nanny soon made herself comfortable, drawing up the sheet to her three chins and yawning, unaware that the metal monster was close at hand, searching for his aspirin!

And, Duckula? He was delving into Nanny's refrigerator, preparing to make himself a sandwich, when Igor walked in.

"Ah, Sir!" he said. "I was just about to bring your spade!"

"A spade, Igor?" cried Duckula, pausing mid-way between half a cucumber and some gorgonzola cheese. "Why would I want a spade?"

"I thought we were to do some burying, Sir . . ." replied Igor, understandably confused.

"No, not berrying, Igor! Berries give me heartburn! What I need is some bread for a tomato, cucumber, lettuce, onion, gorgonzola and ketchup sandwich!"

"You won't be needing the spade then, Sir?"

"No, Igor, I'll spread the butter with a knife!"

Meanwhile, Nanny was sound asleep in Goosewing's laboratory, snoring her head off under the sheet. Goosewing's beady eyes gleamed with excitement when he heard her.

"Ze creature iss alive!" he murmured. "I have done it! Come, mine beauty, rise up for Papa!"

"Chee!" muttered Von Goosewing as Nanny rose up, sleepwalking. "That's the ugliest creature I ever saw! Oh, well, it's too late to be fussy! Come, mine love! Count Duckula must be destroyed!"

At the bottom of the stairs, the real metal monster was pouring his heart out to a suit of armour. "Zo, I was just moved from backyard to backyard . . . It's no life being a trash-can . . ."

"One minute, it's fetch the spade!" broke in Igor's gloomy tones, walking past without even noticing. "Then it's fetch the bread! I wish he'd make up his mind . . ."

"Well, Igor!" a grating voice called out. "Where's the spade?"

"Spade, sir?" Igor's bony old head was spinning. "But, I thought you wanted bread . . ."

"Can't dig a hole with bread, Igor!" came the answer. "No, I must have a spade and quickly! It's nearly dawn!"

"Oh, Sir!" beamed Igor. "You really *are* evil! I knew I was not mistaken!"

Nanny was doing quite well, too, following Von Goosewing's commands to the letter . . .

"Zis way, mine lovely, left right unt left right . . . Now, let me see, was it right here, or left?" Nanny kept on walking . . . "Or perhaps, straight on? I . . ."

"Aaagh!" How Goosewing wished he could control his creation. It really was no fun being trampled on by a non-stop sleep-walker! "Stop! Come back!"

And all this time, poor Duckula had been waiting for Igor to bring the bread for his sandwich!

45

In the end, he decided to go and see where he had got to. So, grabbing a pickled onion – just to keep his strength up – off he went along the corridors, at the same time as his horrible double was taking a stroll from the opposite direction.

It was by sheer chance that they turned to face each other.

"This mirror's filthy!" tutted Duckula, reaching out to give it a rub. His born-again ancestor did the same. "I must tell Igor to clean it!"

"Look at me!" he continued, staring hard at the grey features that faced him. "Sunken eyes . . . and that flabby stomach – yuk! And, as for the face . . . Boy, I need a break!"

"Forgive me for pointing out the obvious," his 'reflection' apologised. "But you do know that vampires have no reflections?"

"Of course, we don't!" snapped Duckula unthinkingly. "Anyone knows that . . ." His words trailed off into a horrified gulp.

"What a beautiful throat you have!" grinned the deadly effigy, baring his fangs with some pride. "And what a neck, just the right size for my teeth!"

"Aaagh . . .!" screamed Duckula. "You've forgotten the orange sauce! Duck should always be served with orange sauce! Wait there and I'll get you some!"

Von Goosewing's monster was still talking to the suit of armour.

"Und I woke up wiz ziss terrible headache, and . . ."

"Help . . .!" interrupted Duckula, fleeing past in the direction of his room. "He-e-e-lp . . .!"

But his evil ancestor was right behind him, crashing in the door and making a grab at Duckula.

"Now my little running buffet!" he roared, baring his fangs once again. "I have you at last!"

"Nanny!" shrieked Duckula in panic. "Nanny! Nanny, he-e-e-lp!" Nanny woke in a flash, brought out of her sleep-walking trance by her master's voice.

"My little Duckyboos!" she cried. "Don't worry! Nanny's coming!" And to prove her point, she burst through the door, sending a shower of splinters and brick-dust into the air.

"Nothing to be afraid of, my darling duck!" she crooned. "Only the sun coming up!"

And even as she spoke, the deadly effigy froze back into a statue, and then crumbled into a pile of rubble.

"There, there my sweetheart," crooned Nanny. "It's alright now."

"Wow!" breathed Duckula at last. "All this excitement has made me hungry! Now, what's happened to Igor and that bread?"

There was no answer. Because Igor was still busy digging the hole for 'his master'.

"Here, little creaturekins!" came Goosewing's voice, horribly close at hand. "Come to Poppa!"

There was an ear-splitting "Aaagh!" as Goosewing fell down the hole – loud enough for Duckula and Nanny to hear as they came downstairs together.

48

"It was a monster, Nanny!" insisted Duckula, recounting his meeting with his horrible ancestor. "A big, ugly thing . . ."

"No," smiled Nanny gently. "You were right in the first place, Duckyboos! There's no such thing as a monster!"

There was a terrible clanking, then a rattling, and a tall figure suddenly loomed in front of them.

"Sorry to trouble you – but you wouldn't happen to have ein aspirin, would you? My poor head's splitting – look!"

"Aaagh . . ." screamed Count Duckula, seeing the jagged split, with all the rusty nuts and bolts inside.

"Aaaaagh . . .!" shrieked Nanny, even louder, taking flight up the castle stairs behind him.

"If you haven't got an aspirin," shouted the monster, "what about one of those zings that go fizz fizz?"

His only answer was another chorus of screams and yells, threatening to echo on through the castle walls until the next stormy night brought its thunder and lightning to Castle Duckula!

4
All in a Fog

Nobody knows the truth behind the grim secrets of Castle Duckula . . .
the dreadful screams, the cries of terror, the sounds of horrifying
instruments of torture . . .

"Oh, Duckyboos . . ." sighed Nanny, as the last notes of Duckula's
organ-playing screeched to a halt. "You've got a lovely touch!"

"Playing helps me concentrate, Nanny!" came the reply. "And I, Count
Duckula, have solved the mystery of the missing cheese grater! Would you
have guessed, the werewolf took it to get a closer shave!"

"Fancy you being a musician, and a detective, Duckyboos!" gushed
Nanny. "Just like that other famous detective!"

"You mean Sherlock Holmes, Nanny?"

"No . . ." said Nanny thoughtfully. "I mean detective . . . Wish I could
think of his name . . ."

"What a great detective needs," proclaimed Duckula, "is strength, a
quick brain, and mastery of a musical instrument!" There was a succession
of out-of-tune chords of the organ. "And, I've got my own magnifying
glass!"

"But, Sir," protested Igor. "No Duckula has ever been on the right side of the law!"

"My mind's made up!" Duckula retorted, already preparing to leap into his favourite coffin and start Castle Duckula on its next journey. "A detective is what I'm going to be! And the only place to be a detective is London, England!"

The sky became streaked with bright yellow and red flashes, as it always did before Castle Duckula shot up into the air – this time, sporting a Union Jack on the top-most turret, all ready to land in Hyde Park!

"Foggy London Town!" announced Igor, peering through the grey gloom. "Rather old hat, don't you think, Milord?"

"Never mind the mist, Igor!" Duckula snapped impatiently. "It's mystery I'm looking for!"

"Hey!" boomed a voice. "There's a sign over there what says Keep Off the Grass! So you can move your flipping castle!"

Igor was most affronted. "Look here," he snarled, "how would you like your arms pulled out, hard boiled, then stuck back again? Because that is precisely what will happen to you, if you don't go away!"

"Oh, well . . ." The man shrank back hurriedly. "Just be out of this park by half past eight, or you'll be locked in!"

"Right!" exclaimed Duckula. "There must be hundreds of crimes waiting to be solved! That's if we can find them in this fog . . ."

"Hallo . . ." came another voice. "Iss zere anybody out zere?"

"Who's that?" called Duckula, hands cupped to his beak.

"Who is zat shouting who's zat?"

"Hello!" Duckula called again, ignoring the accent. "Where are you?"

"Over here!" replied the voice. "Where are you?"

"I'm over here, too!"

"I've a feeling," groaned Igor, "this could be a very long day . . ."

The thick fog also blanketed some curious bleeping noises, . . . Only one person knew they were the signals from a wrist vampireometer – and that was Doctor Von Goosewing, the famous vampire catcher!

"Vat iss zis?" he shrieked. "Zer are vampires close by? Or – could it be zat ziss fog is really Essence of Vampire? I must analyse some in mine analyser!"

Little did he know that Duckula was near, busy being a detective, searching for the missing person in the fog!

"Haaa-aa-ll-ooo . . .!" he yelled. "Oh, it's no good Igor! There must be other crimes going on that have to be solved!"

Quite suddenly, there came the clip-clopping of horses' hooves along the cobbled street, and a Hansom cab loomed ahead.

"Tour of mysterious London, Sir?" growled the cabby, face hidden by a muffler. "Whitechapel, Baker Street, Tower of London! Only a quid!"

"That's only about two thousand Transylvanian Drachmas!" cried Duckula. "What are we waiting for?"

Some distance ahead of Duckula – just outside the Tower of London, to be exact – two strange-looking people were peering through the fog, from a manhole in the pavement.

"Free at last, Mildred!" exclaimed the old man, sniffing the grey air with relish. "Seems like only yesterday we broke in to nick these 'ere crown jewels!"

"It was forty seven years ago, Arthur," his wife reminded him.

"Forty seven years, eh? 'Course, it's the getting out that's been the problem! Anyway, now we can do all we ever wanted!"

"What did we want to do, Arthur?"

"Can't remember . . ." confessed Arthur, pushing his cap back. "Good job I can afford a memory, now!"

" 'Scuse me, young man!" he called, spotting Duckula's yellow beak through the fog. "Mind holding this sack while we gets out of this hole!"

"Well," considered Duckula, automatically handing the sack to Igor, "this isn't quite a mystery . . . But," he continued, beginning to tug at the old man, "I . . . suppose . . . I've . . . got . . . to . . . ooof! start . . . somewhere . . ."

"Allow me, Sir," said Igor. "Nanny – you hold this!"

Nanny obediently held the sack for a few minutes, before bustling forward impatiently.

"Oh, Mister Igor, you're all thumbs!" She thrust the sack towards a tall, pipe-smoking stranger standing nearby. "Here!" she said. "Hold this!"

"Couple of little ones like you shouldn't be too much trouble!" she went on, putting her great arms around both of them. "And . . . Nanny's . . . always . . . careful . . ."

A little more puffing and tugging, one last, desperate pull – and out they popped like a cork from a bottle, falling back in a heap on the pavement, crushed beneath Nanny.

"Oooh!" cried Nanny, then she grabbed the sack from the stranger. "Thank you very much!"

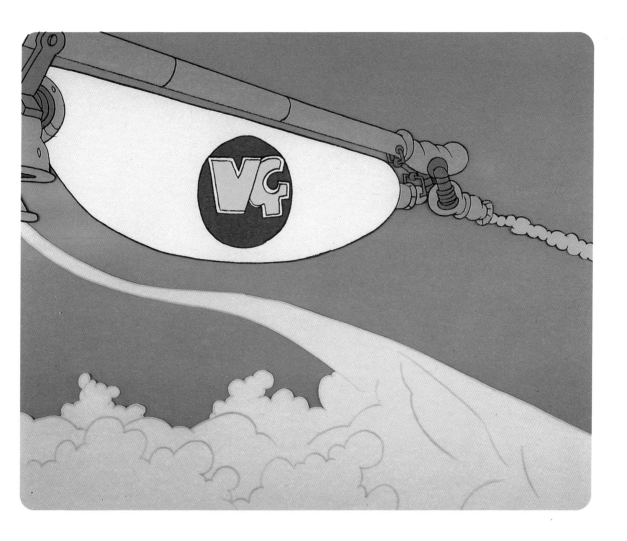

None of them knew it, but, high above London town, Doctor Von Goosewing's airship was on patrol. He seemed very pleased with himself, he was flying in his latest invention – something which looked rather like a giant vacuum cleaner . . .

"Zo!" he cried. "Zis vampire fog zinks it has ze better of Von Goosewing, ja? Vell, I vill prove it wrong vizz mine zuper-duper collector! Now – ver ist der button to start?"

But Goosewing never got anything right first time! The London skies were almost ripped apart by two explosions, neither of which did anything to clear the weather . . .

"Phew!" exclaimed Duckula, wrinkling up his beak at the pipe-smoking stranger. "So you're the one causing all this fog!"

"Mildred, look!" gasped Arthur, as the pipe smoke drifted their way. "It – it's Hawkeye Soames, and his assistant, Potson!"

"Hawkeye Soames?" repeated Duckula blankly.

"I, Sir," said the stranger, "am Hawkeye Soames, Consulting Detective! We have been after the Crown Jewel thieves for years! Now, I am placing you and your manservant under arrest!"

"Arrest?" Duckula staggered back a few paces. "What for?"

"For being accomplices to the master criminal – namely, one large one-armed hen. Probably a domestic of some sort by profession who . . ."

"Wow – how did you deduce that?" gasped Duckula.

"Because she is standing there holding a sack of jewels."

"Amazing, Soames!" gasped Potson, most impressed.

"But I didn't steal any jewels!" wailed Nanny. "I'm too stupid!"

"That's right, Soames!" Igor confirmed solemnly. "She is very, very stupid!"

Nanny beamed so delightedly that all three chins wobbled at once. "I knew I could rely on you, Mister Igor! Here, you'd better have it back, now!" She handed Igor the sack.

"So!" burst out Soames, pointing an accusing finger at Igor, clutching the sack. "You are the culprit!"

"Brilliant, Soames!" put in Potson. "The butler did it!"

"Give me a break!" cried Igor, falling to his knees. "It was my master who gave me this sack!"

"Igor!" scolded Duckula. "I *will* give you the sack when this is over. How can you behave like a pathetic coward?"

"Years of practice, Sir . . ." droned Igor.

"Anyway," continued Duckula, "this sack belongs to them . . . Hey!" He looked around for some sign of Arthur and Mildred. "Where are they? Those two little people who came out of the ground . . ."

"Most unconvincing, Sir," replied Soames. "I'd advise you to come quietly!"

Meanwhile, Von Goosewing had been working hard until his invention seemed to be perfectly under control.

"Just a little more juice," he muttered, peering down in the general direction of the jail, "unt away we are going!"

Duckula meanwhile was sulking in a damp prison cell with Igor and Nanny.

"Soames," Igor kept saying, "you are making a grave mistake!"

"And if anyone knows about graves," put in Nanny, "it's Mister Igor!"

"Fog seems to be lifting, Soames!" observed Potson, ignoring Nanny.

"So it does, Potson," agreed Soames. "So it does!"

But, not only the fog was lifting . . . Before long, park benches, pillar boxes, litter-bins . . . all floated skywards, sucked up by Von Goosewing's marvellous vampire fog-catching invention!

"Come, Potson!" said Soames, holding up the sack of jewels. "These must now be returned . . .!"

"Crown jewels!" bellowed Potson, seeing them shooting up into the sky. "Come back, I say, or . . . Aaaagh . . .!"

"Stop!" yelled Soames, making a desperate grab at Potson's ankles, but to no avail. "Return my assistant at once!"

"I think," said Duckula, glancing up to see the top of the prison cell fast disappearing, "it's probably best if we leave now, Igor!"

"Yes, Sir," Igor agreed hurriedly. "While the going's g . . ."

"While the going's g . . .?" echoed Nanny. "That doesn't make sense, Mister Igor! Mister Igor . . . Aaaagh . . .!"

"You know," Goosewing muttered to himself, "I could swear dat fog looked like a great ugly hen with her arm in unt sling! Perhaps I have been working too hard . . ."

His invention certainly was working too hard! First, the Tower of London went, brick by brick. Then, Nelson's Column . . . Buckingham Palace . . . The Waxworks Museum . . . Even Arthur and Mildred's front room – complete with Arthur and Mildred, whilst they were congratulating themselves on making a successful get-away!

"Zere is no stop button!" screeched Goosewing, rushing around and working all the switches at once. "Zo, I must get zer machinery into some kind of backwards reverse movement!"

He siezed the biggest lever he could find and pulled hard with both hands. Almost immediately, there was a loud blast of air.

"Chee!" wailed Goosewing. "Now, voss izz happening?"

Bricks . . . pillar boxes . . . benches . . . people . . . bits of The Tower of London and Buckingham Palace . . . Everything was being shot out from the giant nozzle of Von Goosewing's machine – and landing in all the wrong places!

Whoever heard of a pipe-smoking detective at the top of Nelson's Column?

"You down there!" roared Soames. "Stop, in the name of the law!"

"D'you think he means us, Mildred?" wondered Arthur, kicking a motor-bike into action.

"Leave it to a real detective, Soames!" advised Duckula, with a short laugh. "Cab!"

Duckula chased Arthur and Mildred all over London, past Buckingham Palace, with the "WAXWORKS" notice over the door, and through the shops floating on the Serpentine, pausing only to admire Mildred's three piece suite which was now at The Tower of London. Only one thing was missing . . .

"Somezink is stuck in der machinery!" announced Von Goosewing, and gave it a hefty bash.

"Ah!" Goosewing cried, seeing a television set shooting out into the air with quite a flourish. "Zat gives me indigestion, too!"

The television landed right in front of Arthur and Mildred, making their motor-bike skid to a halt.

"Caught at last!" yelled Duckula triumphantly. "Hand over the jewels, or I'll get Nanny to surround you!"

"Ssssh . . .!" hissed Arthur. "Not while our favourite programme's on! It's Duckula, you know!"

"Trust this rotten Castle to spoil things!" complained Count Duckula from the T.V. screen. "Just when I was about to become famous! Only one thing can make me happy, now!"

"Oh, no, Sir!" pleaded Igor. "Please, I beg of you, think again . . .!"

But his words fell on deaf ears. Which was just as well, as Duckula had begun playing the organ again – this time, accompanying the chimes of Big Ben, which had so recently been added to the East Wing . . .